This book belongs to:

. . . .

For Mum, Dad, Bina and 'H'.
Ranjit

For Yara, Nora, Melody, Nona, Narvan, Borna, Misha and all the little ones with big imaginations!
Mehrdokht

First published in the United Kingdom in 2018 by Lantana Publishing Ltd., London.
www.lantanapublishing.com

American edition published in 2018 by Lantana Publishing Ltd., UK.
info@lantanapublishing.com

Text © Ranjit S. Dhaliwal 2018
Illustration © Mehrdokht Amini 2018

Distributed in the United States and Canada by Lerner Publishing Group, Inc.
241 First Avenue North, Minneapolis, MN 55401 U.S.A.
For reading levels and more information, look for this title at www.lernerbooks.com.
Cataloging-in-Publication Data Available.

Printed and bound in Hong Kong.

ISBN: 978-1-911373-24-7
eBook ISBN: 978-1-911373-25-4

Nimesh the Adventurer

Ranjit Singh   Mehrdokht Amini

LANTANA PUBLISHING

Hello Nimesh,
is school over?

School? My friend, this
is not a school! It's an
ancient cave, and shhhh!
Or you'll wake...

...the DRAGON!

Now we arrive at the bottom of the ocean.

It looks like a corridor to me, Nimesh.

Corridor? Why would a corridor be full of...

Are you going down this road, Nimesh?

Road? What road? My friend, we have reached...

...the North Pole!

Look at these glaciers of ice! Hear those avalanches of snow!

Can you feel the ground tremble?

Watch as I skate across the ice
with my sleigh of dogs!

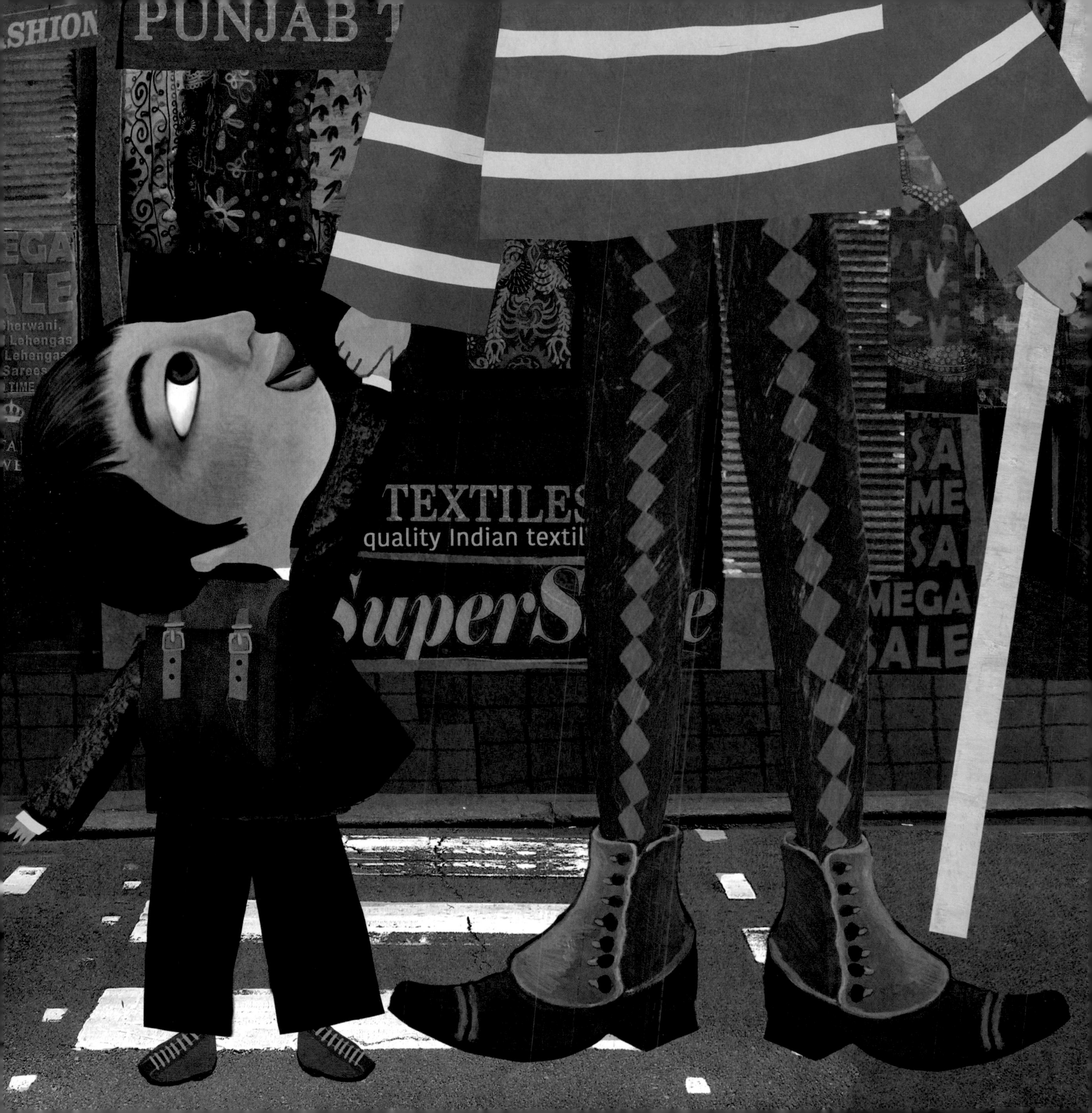
SHION
PUNJAB T
TEXTILES
quality Indian textil
MEGA
SALE

...a guardsman for the Indian Maharaja.

Oh really, Nimesh?

Oh yes, he told me so. He once backflipped right across the Maharaja's table...

...and didn't even smash or break anything!

We'll find a beach behind those palm trees.

No, we'll find the local park, Nimesh.

And what's this, Nimesh?

Is it a cave full of gold?
Or an emperor's castle?
Perhaps a lush forest?

This is home.